LION

BENJAMIN HULME-CROSS

Illustrated by
Nelson Evergreen

First published 2014 by A & C Black,
an imprint of Bloomsbury Publishing Plc
50 Bedford Square
London WC1B 3DP
Bloomsbury is a registered trademark of Bloomsbury Publishing Plc

www.bloomsbury.com

ISBN 978-1-4729-0099-9

A CIP catalogue for this book is available from the British Library.

Printed and bound in India by Replika Press Pvt Ltd

1 3 5 7 9 10 8 6 4 2

The Teens can choose prison for life … or they can go on a game show called The Caves.

If the Teens beat the robot monsters, they go free. If they lose, they die.

I am Zak. Sometimes I help the Teens. Sometimes I don't.

The Teens were called Emma and Bee.
They looked small. They ran to the caves.

The Voice spoke.

"The game begins in 10 minutes."

I went after them into the caves.

They didn't see me.

Emma was crying.

Emma said, "It's not fair. That man told lies about us. We didn't do it!"

"The police lied too. Nobody listened to us,"
said Bee.

I thought the Teens were telling the truth.

I took a spear and a knife out of my bag and put them on the ground.

Then I went back outside.

There was a cage on the rocks. There was a huge lion inside the cage. It growled.

The cage door opened. The lion ran out.

I went back into the caves. I ran to the girls.
They held the weapons.

"It's a lion," I said. "It's coming now."

They looked scared.

"You can kill it. Make sure it doesn't see you,"
I said. "You must help each other."

"Will you help us?" said Bee.

"I have helped you," I said.

We heard a low growl.

"Quick!" said Bee. "Be brave, Emma!"

I climbed up the walls of the cave. Bee climbed up the wall after me.

Emma stood with the spear pointing at the tunnel.

Bee climbed around the walls. She waited on the rocks above the tunnel.

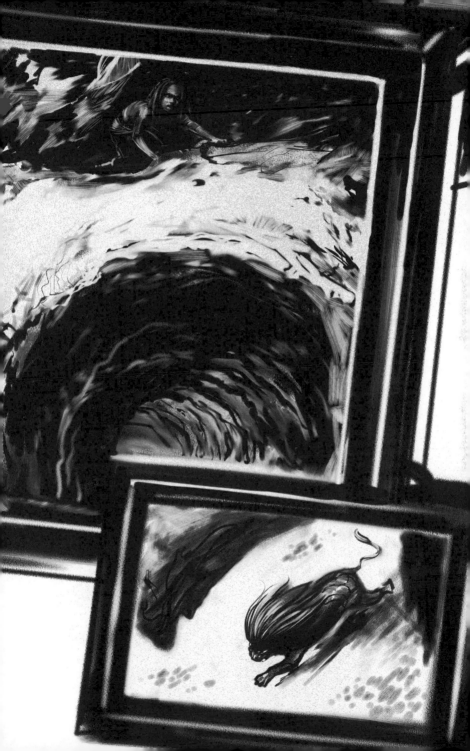

The lion came through the tunnel.

It walked into the cave. It looked at Emma.

It showed its teeth.

The lion roared. Emma waited. The lion came closer. Emma threw the spear at it.

The lion hit the spear with its paw. The spear fell to the ground. Emma screamed. Now she had no weapon.

Bee jumped down onto the lion's back. She hit the lion with the knife. The knife went into the lion's neck.

The lion fell to the ground.
It was dead.

The Voice said,
"Game over!"

Read more of

THE

CAVES

SERIES